FUNIMALS

Written by Paul Rogers

Illustrated by Charles Fuge

BARRON'S
NEW YORK

What's this animal? Do you know?

A buffalump or a buffalo?

Flipping its wings and waddling along –
A penguin or a pingopong?

Scaly skin and a nasty smile –
A crocosnap or a crocodile?

Stretching its claws and swishing its tail –
A tiger or a stripingale?

A jungle bird that can learn to talk –
A parrot or a parrosquawk?

Holding paws in the icy air –
A roly-pole or a polar bear?

An ugly face from the day it was born –
A rhino or a runcihorn?

Taking a ride on its mother's back –

A koala or a carryjack?

Born with a big warm coat to wear –
A groozle or a grizzly bear?

Sharp as a needle, each prickly spine –
A porcupuss or a porcupine?

Taller than all the others by half—

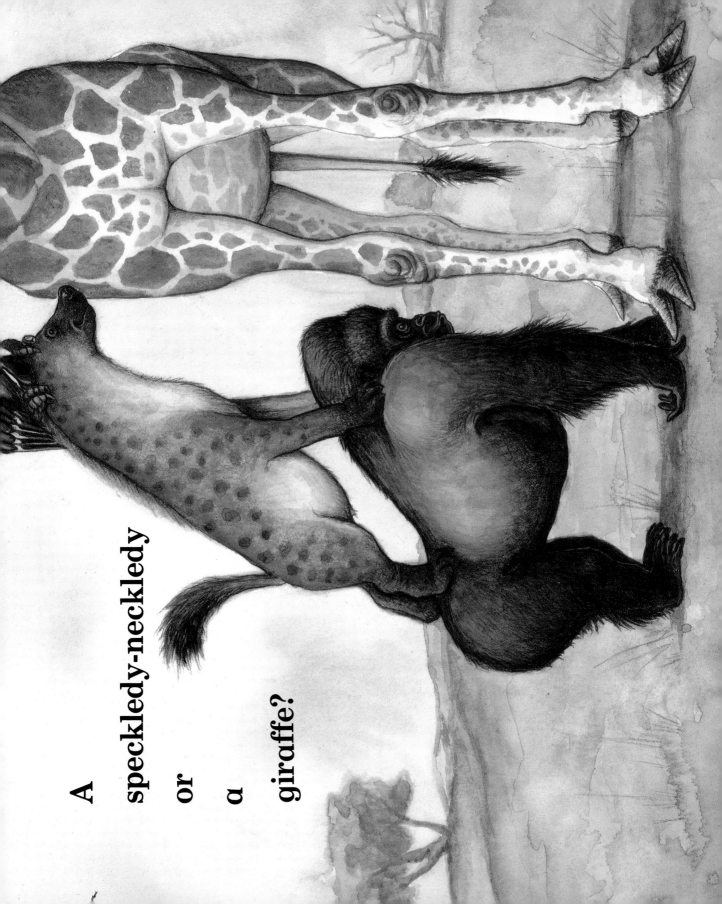

A
speckledy-neckledy
or
a
giraffe?

Big black eyes and ears to match –
A panda or a paddypatch?

A bit like you and a bit like me –
A chimpanzoo or a chimpanzee?

For Mark Infield P.R.
For Karen C.F.

First edition for the United States published 1991
by Barron's Educational Series Inc.

Text copyright © Paul Rogers 1991
Illustrations copyright © Charles Fuge 1991

First published in Great Britain in 1991 by
The Bodley Head Children's Books an Imprint of
the Random Century Group, Ltd.

All inquiries should be addressed to:
Barron's Educational Series, Inc.
250 Wireless Boulevard
Hauppauge, New York 11788

Library of Congress Catalog Card No.90-23340
International Standard Book No. 0-8120-6216-7

Library of Congress Cataloging-in-Publication Data

Rogers, Paul, 1950

    Funimals/written by Paul Rogers: illustrated by Charles
Fuge.
    1st ed. for the United States.
      p. cm.

    "First published in Great Britain in 1991 by the
    Bodley Head
Children's Books" T.p. verso.

    Summary: Presents illustrations of a parade of animals whose
appearance or behavior suggests appropriate alternate names.

    ISBN 0-8120-6216-7

    [1. Animals – Fiction. 2. Stories in rhyme.] I. Fuge, Charles,
Ill. II. Title.

PZ8.3.R645FU 1991
[E] – dc20   90-23340   CIP

Printed in Hong Kong
  1234   987654321